To my loving husband and children who mean the world to me and inspire everything I do.

– Caroline Peters

www.mascotbooks.com

For more information, please contact:
Mascot Books
560 Herndon Parkway #120
Herndon, VA 20170
info@mascotbooks.com

CPSIA Code: PRT0613A
ISBN-10: 1620862700
ISBN-13: 9781620862704

Printed in the United States

A is for Aspen Trees
With shades so pretty and bright.
The leaves change colors in the Fall
It's really quite a sight!

B is for Biking
Push down on your pedals.
Many olympians train here
Aspiring for gold medals.

C is for Cave of the Winds
An incredible world underground.
Take a discovery or lantern tour
There is so much to be found!

D is for Denver
A mile above the sea.
This city is the state capital.
It's beautiful…you'll see!

E is for Elk
Wild mountain game.
Look and observe
But don't try to tame.

F is for Fly Fishing
In Colorado's tranquil streams.
Wear your waders, bring your rods,
This sport can be extreme.

G is for Garden of the Gods
A National Natural Landmark.
With towering rock formations to see
This place you will want to embark.

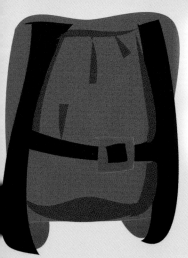

H is for Hiking
In the Colorado Wilderness.
Animals to see, mountains to climb,
The possibilities are endless.

I is for Ice Castles in Steamboat Springs
A place that will spark our imagination
As we crawl through turquoise tunnels
And gaze at a spectacular ice formation.

J is for John Denver
A famous performer and musician.
He sang "Rocky Mountain High."
Be sure and take a listen.

K is for Kayak
Through the rushing water so swift.
Hold on to your paddles
So you won't need a lift!

L is for Landscape
Panoramic views for miles around.
Mountains, forests, and deserts,
A prettier picture can't be found.

M is for Music
Live shows with singing and jazz.
Come see a concert at Red Rocks
You'll be filled with pizzazz!

N is for the Nuggets
Watch these basketball players score!
See them dunk, see them win,
Hear the crowds roar!

O is for Ouray Hot Springs
We'll swim and splash around
And watch the glistening mineral pools
As steam rises from the ground.

P is for Pizza!
So cheesy, yummy, and hot.
After a day of adventure
It'll sure hit the spot!

Q is for Quite a lot to do
Skiing and snowboarding are so fun.
Let's catch the chairlift one more time
And squeeze in one last run!

R is for Rocky Mountains
So glorious and grand.
From up here you'll see
the best views in the land!

S is for Skiing
Down the mountain so fast.
Bring your friends and family
We'll all have a blast!

T is for Trout
These fish are so quick.
Watch out if you catch one.
Their scales are oh so slick!

U is for the U.S. Air Force Academy
Where cadets train to be the best.
They serve, work hard, and prepare
So, in peace, we can rest.

V is for Vacation
There are so many mountain towns.
Visit Crested Butte, Vail, Aspen, or Beaver Creek.
You'll never see a frown.

W is for Whitewater Rafting
Down the rapids we'll go fast.
Hurry! Paddle quickly!
We don't want to finish last!

X is for eXcellent
The best time it will be
Visit in summer, spring, winter, or fall.
There is so much to see!

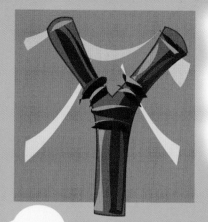

Y is for Yurt
A teepee to sleep in while you camp.
Waking up to a cool summer morning
You'll feel like a champ!

Z is for the Zoo in Cheyenne Mountain
Where you can see grizzly bears up close!
My favorites are the moose and mountain lions.
Which ones do you like the most?

Traveling with you was so much fun!
We learned a lot and stayed very busy.
If you'd like to take another great trip,
My twin sister, Madeline, will show you New York City!

About the Author

Caroline Peters graduated from the University of Texas in Austin. She currently lives in Houston with her husband and three children. She is a former kindergarten teacher and continues to have a passion for teaching young children. An avid traveler, she was inspired to create an alphabet series to help make teaching fun!